1500

Globish Words
for International Communication

全球化英語時代
必備 **1500** 單字

Q&A Globish 全球化英語

Q: 為什麼要用 Globish?

A: 全球化時代來臨,我們不只是和英文母語人士溝通,而是和世界各國的人士開啓對話,因此我們需要大家都能彼此溝通無礙的基礎語言。這種強調功能性,以非母語人士為主的英語,多位學者專家稱之為全球化英語(Globish 或 Global English)。

Q: 什麼是 Globish?

A: Globish 的四大特色:

- 只要 1500 個英文單字就能輕鬆溝通
- 使用簡單而正確的英文句子就好
- 發音、拼字不必多背,1500 單字以及延伸字就足以使用
- 無論商務洽公、業務推廣、旅遊觀光,都可以用 Globish 這個工具達成溝通目的

Q: 誰是 Globish 的提倡者?

A: 奈易耶 Jean-Paul Nerriere、大衛洪 David Hon

奈易耶是 IBM 公司歐洲中東非洲區的副總裁,曾在美國總部擔任副總裁,負責全球行銷業務,每天都必須使用英語,也觀察到一些規則。奈易耶跨越全球的工作經驗讓他看見解決全球溝通問題只有一個大家都想不到的方法,那就是Globish。

大衛洪擁有英語碩士學位,在南美教過英文,曾發展出全球第一套醫學模擬器,獲得多項獎項,創立 Ixion 公司。當他看到了奈易耶提出的概念,覺得這就是他想要主張的概念,因此展開了合作。

Q: Globish 有何效應？

A: Globish 觀念一出後，引發各界的關注與報導，美國 *Newsweek* 曾以封面故事介紹 Globish 概念。各國各大媒體亦爭相報導，日本、韓國各大企業執行長要求員工必須具備基本英文能力。

Q: 如何更了解 **Globish** 的觀念？

A: 有關 Globish 的觀念，可參閱由奈易耶 Jean-Paul Nerriere 與大衛洪 David Hon 所合著的 *Globish: The World Over*《全球化英語：輕鬆和全世界溝通》一書，了解更多有關 Globish 的重要概念。（中英對照版‧聯經出版）

「背生字」是台灣學生從小到大學習英語必備的基本功夫，常見學生在公車或捷運上，手持一小本手抄或印製的生字本，口中念念有詞的背誦著，這些生字可能是當天會考的單字，也可能是指考或英文檢定測驗的生字範圍，總之背生字長久以來是增進英語能力的不二法門，無怪乎學生嫌自己英文不好的理由，十之八九，總怪自己英文生字背得不夠多，似乎英文生字記得越多，英文應該就會跟著好起來。

既然多數的觀念都是生字的多寡影響英文學習成效及英文考試績效，坊間許多英語學習書都是以英語字彙為號召，例如：教育部所頒布的《九年一貫英語教學課程標準常用1200 字彙》，《全民英檢高級 1500 字彙》、《國中小基本 2000 字彙》……到書店英語學習書的部門走一圈，放眼看去，幾乎都是英文單字書。和其他單字書不同的是，《全球化英語時代必備 1500 單字》不是以考試為取向，讀者若翻開書後的 1500 單字表，或許感到很疑惑？選擇這些單字的標準依據是什麼？

當初 Globish 創始團隊揀選這 1500 單字是有感於英語語系的國家的傳媒用語十分艱深，完全無視於外國人學習英文的痛苦。Globish 創始者Jean-Paul Nerriere 是法國人，1965 年起在 IBM 電腦公司任職 27 年間，常在世界各地業務考察，據他觀察，非英語人士相互之間可以毫不費力地用簡單的英語談生意、話家常，於是他大聲呼籲：欲使英語成為真正的通行世界的語言，大家都應該廣泛使用簡而有力的單字和句子，在他看來，只要熟悉 Globish1500 單字用法，用英語溝通當易如反掌。

揀選這 1500 個單字並非易事，首先由 Globish 團隊每日公司內部日誌開始身體力行，同仁用最簡單的字書寫工作日誌，並相互校閱，看是否有更簡單的字可以取代日誌中的某些字彙。經年累月下來，選出了 195 個常用字，接著再加上 500 個單字，其中 76 字是美語中常用名稱、127 字來自美國常用食物名、186 字來自商業常用語、111 字來動、植物名。另外 700 字則來自於字典（*The Penguin Roget's College Thesaurus in Dictionary Form*）

筆者當初編寫這本 Globish1500 單字書時，不想違背 Globish 精神與初衷，既然簡單的字彙是需要活用的，所以不必拘泥於以 A、B、C、D…… 單字的排列順序，用一個

單字配一個句子，而是將生字群分為 14 個主題來呈現。14 個主題多來自筆者逢甲大學畢業生的建議，這些學生畢業後到各行各業職場上工作，他們有些時候需要用英文自我介紹、用英文作簡報、用英文取消訂單、或用英文向人道賀、致歉或致哀……等等，這些場景其實都可以用 Globish1500 單字清楚表達出來。

為了使 Globish 1500 單字更精準地表達各種場景中複雜的概念，我邀請美國哥倫比亞新聞研究所畢業的 Miranda Lin 與我合寫《全球化英語時代必備 1500 單字》。英語是 Miranda Lin 的母語，他曾在紐約大小報紙撰寫新聞稿，對職場用語毫不陌生，我們通篇只用 Globish 1500 單字便完成了各個場景的電子郵件篇、電話篇、口語篇、和簡報篇。每一課的每個單字，我們都列出不同的解釋與用法，以及該單字常用的詞類變化，其實，這也正是英文字複雜的地方，以三個 Globish 的生字為例：

● place 這個簡單的字可以當名詞，意指「地方」，也可以當動詞，意指「放置」，如 place a book on the table（放書在桌上）。還可以指「下訂單」place an order。

● stand 可以當動詞，意指「站立」，也可以當名詞意指「立場」，如 What is your stand?（你的立場是什麼？）

● ship 這個自當名詞時是「船」，當動詞時意指「運送」。它延伸的兩個名詞則是：shipping（運貨）和 shipment（出貨）

所以看似簡單的 1500 單字，其實每個字都有深意。讀者不需要死背這些單字的中文意思，只需要瞭解並熟悉每個單字在不同場景的用法即可。

和 Miranda Lin 合寫完這本書，我們都很感謝一位中英文俱佳的加拿大工程師 Charles Lin 幫我們悉心逐字校對，並提供中肯意見。讀者在研讀此書時若遇到任何問題，請寫信給我：wentingshu@gmail.com，我一定立即回答。最後希望《全球化英語時代必備 1500 單字》這本攜帶方便的書，可以使讀者真正活用單字而不是死背單字的技巧，使職場的尖兵遇到英語書信或口語溝通的難題，都能在書中找到答案。

文庭澍

As a writer born and raised in Canada, I used to take languages for granted. Although both of my grand-parents were the first generation immigrants from Taiwan, English was my first language and it was never something I had to study; I simply said and wrote what's "felt" right.

在雙語的加拿大出生長大的我，曾以為語言的運用是再自然不過的事了。雖然我的祖父母是從台灣來的第一代移民，但英文是我的第一語言，我不需要「讀」英文，只需要「憑感覺」來說、來寫英文。

Then in the fall of 2011, I moved to Beijing, China to begin studying Mandarin-Chinese. It was my first time learning a new language and the first time I had to consciously think about how words and sentences were put together. It was also the first time I felt challenged by language.

2011 年我特地到北京去學中文，這是我第一次去學一個陌生的語言，第一次需要特別思考，如何把單字和句子組合起來。這也是我第一次感覺到語言對我的挑戰。

Like many of you, I spent hours both in and outside of class glued to my textbooks, diligently memorizing the vocabulary lists and grammar lessons. I bought additional dictionaries and reference books and mp3 discs so that every moment could be devoted to absorbing more words. According to our teachers, by the end of the year we had learned over 3,000 new words.

就像各位讀者一樣，我在中文課堂上以及課外時間盯著課本、認真地背生字、默默地記文法，還買了許多字典、參考書和 MP3 光碟，我沒有放棄任何一刻可以增加中文字彙的時間。老師說到這個學期，我們已經認識了 3000 個新的中文字詞。

But I soon realized that while I may have studied 3,000 new words, I did not know how to use 3,000 words. As soon as I put down my textbook and tried to engage with other people, I became confused and tongue-tied. I had crammed thousands of words and phrases into my brain, but had no idea which ones were appropriate for what situation.

但我很快發現即使學了 3000 個中文新字，卻不知道該如何去應用這 3000 個新字。一旦放下課本，要去跟人溝通的時候，我就傻了眼、舌頭一直打結。即使腦袋裡已經裝進了幾千個字詞，我卻不清楚到底在哪些場合可以應用哪幾個字詞。

The experience was frustrating, but also enlightening.

這個教人氣餒的經歷卻也給了我一個新的啟示。

Language is not about memorizing the largest number of words; it's about the ability to communicate and interact with other people. My co-author Wen Ting-shu and I therefore tried to avoid simply giving you yet another long list of terms that you had no idea how to apply to your daily life.

學習語言不是去背誦最多的字詞，而是如何增強與人溝通的能力。文庭澍女士和我合作編寫這本書的目的　不是再給你一長串的英文生字清單，或一些無法在日常生活中運用的生字。

Instead, we started by creating the scenarios you are likely to encounter in your everyday life, and then chose the words needed to handle those situations. From organizing meetings to emailing your boss to just recommending a good restaurant to your friend, we have attempted to provide a vocabulary that you will actually need and use.

我們先編排出日常生活裡常會遇到的狀況，然後搭配選出需要用到的字詞。這些情境從安排會議、到發電子郵件，或是向朋友推薦一家不錯的餐館等等，我們選擇的字詞都是在情境表達中，和他人溝通所必要用的字詞。

Many of the 1,500 selected words may seem simple or even below your skill level, but that is precisely the point. These are not words that need to be tediously memorized, but rather ones that are already familiar and thus can be easily employed in various situations.

這 1500 英文單字中，有些字看似簡單，甚至低於你的程度，但這正是溝通效能的核心所在。這些熟悉的字詞，你不須再花功夫去記誦，我們希望你在適當場合能夠很輕鬆地使用出來。

By focusing on basic but necessary words – and most importantly on how to use them practically – we hope we can make studying English useful, accessible, and enjoyable.

當務之急是把注意力集中在這 1500 個基本但卻是絕對必要的英文字詞上，並且實地活用單字。我們的目標是要幫助大家快樂地學習，靈活、有效地使用英文。

Miranda Lin
林家瑞

目次 Table of Contents

目次 Table of Contents

Chapter 1

Making Introductions
介紹新進人員/自我介紹

日常生活中我們有時需要向初次見面的人介紹自己，有些場合我們需要介紹朋友們彼此認識、有時則需要介紹新進員工給其他同仁認識……這些都可以用簡單的 **Globish** 單字達成任務。

I. Introducing a New Co-Worker（Email Version）
介紹新員工（電子郵件篇）

Yasmin 是銀行分行主管，Derek Tam 是新進業務員，請看這位主管如何介紹這位新手給辦公室同仁認識：

🎧 01

Dear co-workers,

I want you to meet Derek Tam, our new sales **representative** for the Wanfang **branch**.

Derek is **fresh** out of college and just **completed** his **degree** at the National Taiwan University with a **joint major** in finance and **politics**. Before joining us, Derek was a summer **trainee** at ABC Company and **supervised** a children's education program for the mayor's office.

We feel very lucky to have Derek **on board**, but we will need the whole office's **support** over the next few weeks to help him get **settled in** to his new **position** and caught up to **speed** on all his **responsibilities**.

If anyone (**including** you, Derek) has any questions, please feel free to **reach** out to me any time.

Welcome to the team, Derek!

Yasmin

中譯

同仁們，各位好，

讓我介紹新上任的業務員 Derek Tam，他將為我們萬芳分行工作。

Derek 剛從大學畢業，在台灣大學取得的學位是財政金融和政治學雙主修。在加入我們公司之前，他在 ABC 公司當暑期實習生，為市政府主辦兒童教育的工作。

我們很幸運有 Derek 加入我們的行列，但我們需要辦公室所有的同仁支持，幫他在下面幾個禮拜內熟習新職，並很快能接上所有工作上的職責。

如果任何人(包括你 Derek 在內)，有任何問題，請不要客氣，隨時跟我聯絡。
Derek，歡迎加入我們的團隊！

Yasmin

 Globish 單字

 02

1. represent 代表（動詞）

例句：He will represent our company and attend the meeting.

中譯：他將代表我們公司參加會議。

 延伸　**representative** 代表（名詞）

例句：He is our new sales representative.

中譯：他是我們公司新進業務員。

2. branch 分店、分公司、部門（名詞）

例句：He was sent to a different branch of the government.

中譯：他被派到一個不同的政府單位。

延伸　**branch out** 擴展不同的工作（動詞）

例句：He branched out from international trade into insurance.

中譯：他從國貿擴展到保險業務。

3. fresh 新鮮的（形容詞）

例句：The vegetables were fresh from the garden.

中譯：這些新鮮蔬菜是從菜園裡摘的。

fresh out of 剛從

例句：She's lucky she found a job fresh out of business school.

中譯：她很幸運，剛從商學院畢業就找到了工作。

---

4. complete 完成（動詞）

例句：Once you complete your training, you can begin working on your own.

中譯：一旦你受訓完畢後，就可以開始獨立作業了。

complete 完成（形容詞）

例句：All my in-house training was complete.

中譯：我的所有在職訓練都已完畢。

5. degree 程度、學位（名詞）

例句：I agree with you to some degree.

中譯：某種程度上來說，我同意你。

例句：She earned her master's degree when she was 23 years old.

中譯：她 23 歲時拿到碩士學位。

6. joint 關節（名詞）

例句：His joints started to hurt more as he became older.

中譯：他年紀漸大，關節開始更痛了。

joint 聯合的（形容詞）

例句：After they got married, they opened a joint bank account.

中譯：結婚之後，他們開了一個聯名戶頭。

7. major 主修、系（名詞）

例句：His major in college is psychology.

中譯：他在大學的主修是心理。

major 主要的（形容詞）

例句：A major part of his job was filing documents.

中譯：他主要的工作是將資料歸檔。

> **major in** 讀……系（動詞）
>
> 例句：What are you majoring in?
>
> 中譯：你讀什麼系？

8. politics 政治（名詞）

例句：Most young people in Taiwan are not interested in politics.

中譯：大多數的台灣年輕人對政治都沒興趣。

> **political** 政治的（形容詞）
>
> 例句：Her political views are pretty left-wing.
>
> 中譯：她政治的觀點很左派。

9. train 火車（名詞）

例句：What time is the last train to London?

中譯：到倫敦的最後一班車是幾點？

train 訓練（動詞）

例句：They were trained to be good citizens.

中譯：他們被訓練成良好公民。

> **trainer** 教練、培訓員
>
> 例句：She has been a teacher trainer for many years.
>
> 中譯：她當師資培訓員已有多年。
>
> **trainee** 實習生、受訓生
>
> 例句：This company needs 5 trainees to work in the summer.
>
> 中譯：這家公司夏天需要 5 名實習生工作。

10. supervise 指導、監督（動詞）

例句：The professor supervises the students doing research in the laboratory.

中譯：這位教授指導學生在實驗室裡做研究。

 supervisor 指導教授

例句：Her supervisor has published ten papers this year.

中譯：她的指導教授今年發表了 10 篇學術文章。

11. board 董事會（名詞）

例句：The board members voted to cut the budget next year.

中譯：董事投票削減了明年度的預算。

board 登上（交通工具）（動詞）

例句：It's almost time to depart; everyone please board the bus now.

中譯：發車時間快到了，請大家上巴士。

 boarding pass 登機證

例句：The gate number is on your boarding pass.

中譯：登機門號寫在你的登機證上。

on board 成為……的一員

例句：He made sure everyone was on board with his idea before proposing it to the committee.

中譯：他確定每個人都同意他的看法後才將意見提交給委員會。

room and board 食宿

例句：The fee does not cover the cost of room and board.

中譯：這些費用並不包括你的食宿費。

12. support 支持（名詞）

例句：I can count on his support for my campaign.

中譯：我的競選活動可以靠他支持。

support 支持（動詞）

例句：She has to work two jobs in order to support her family.

中譯：他必須做兩份工作來養家。

 moral support 道義支持，精神支柱

例句：There is not much I can do, but I can give you some moral support.

中譯：我幫不了什麼忙，但我會給你一些精神支柱。

supportive 支持的（形容詞）

例句：All the staff in our company are very supportive of this project.

中譯：所有的員工都很支持這項計畫案。

13. settle 搞定、解決（動詞）

例句：They asked him to settle the pay dispute.

中譯：他們請他去解決這場工資糾紛。

 settle in 習慣

例句：When you move to a new office, it may take a few weeks to settle in.

中譯：當你換新工作，可能需要幾個禮拜才能習慣。

settle down 安定、安頓

例句：They got married and settled down in a small town.

中譯：他們結了婚，在一個小鎮上安頓下來。

14. position 職位（名詞）

例句：I am not in a position to give out the names of our new staff.

中譯：我的職位還輪不到我交出新進職員的名單。

15. speed 速度（名詞）

例句：Our freeway's speed limit is 100 km/h.

中譯：我們高速公路的速限是每小時100公里。

speed 加速（動詞）

例句：We had better speed up the manufacturing process.

中譯：我們最好加快製作過程。

 up to speed 趕得上進度

例句：After the holidays, he needed to be brought up to speed again on all the new developments.

中譯：假期過後，我們得幫他趕上各方面的進度。

16. responsible 負責任的（形容詞）

例句：They are responsible for quality control in the factory.

中譯：他們負責工廠的品管。

 responsibility 責任（名詞）

例句：It's my daughter's responsibility to make sure all the documents are filed on time.

中譯：我女兒的職責是核實辦公室所有的文件都能如期歸檔。

17. include 包括（動詞）

例句：This price includes food and drinks.

中譯：花費包括食物和飲料。

18. reach 到達、延伸（動詞）

例句：The money needs six working days to reach your bank account.

中譯：錢需要六個工作天才能到你的銀行戶頭裡。

19. welcome 歡迎（名詞）

例句：The company gave him a warm welcome by organizing a party just for him.

中譯：公司為他開了一個派對，給予他熱烈的歡迎。

welcome 歡迎（動詞）

例句：I always welcome a challenge.

中譯：我們總是喜歡接受挑戰。

welcome 受歡迎的（形容詞）

例句：Everyone in the office tried to make him feel welcome.

中譯：辦公室的每個人上前去歡迎他。

II. Introducing Yourself to Co-workers （Email Version）
跟同仁自我介紹（電子郵件篇）

現在輪到 **Derek Tam** 來自我介紹：

 03

Hi everyone,

Thank you so much for the warm welcome. I am so happy to be a part of the team at Hua Tung Bank.

My father was also an employee at Hua Tung for 25 years, and so growing up I always thought of this bank as a **symbol** of success and **opportunity**.

As Yasmin said, I am currently **stationed** at the Wanfang branch. My main **task** will be to work with small and **independent** businesses.

On a less **serious** note though, besides work, I also enjoy reading books, traveling, and swimming, and I was a **former** dance teacher in college.

If anyone would like to reach me, my phone extension is 1234 and my email address is dtam@htbank.com.tw.

Looking forward to working with all of you soon,

Derek

 中譯

各位同仁，

謝謝你們的熱烈歡迎，我很高興成為華東銀行的一員。

我父親曾在華東服務 25 年，成長的過程中我總覺得華東銀行象徵著成功和機會。

如老闆所言，我目前在萬芳分行工作，我工作的範圍是為小型獨資企業服務。

換個輕鬆的話題，除了工作之外，我喜歡閱讀、旅遊和游泳，我過去還是大學的舞蹈老師。

如果您想跟我聯絡，我辦公室的分機是 1234，我的電子郵件信箱是：
dtam@htbank.com.tw

期待很快與各位同仁一起工作。

Derek

Globish
單字

 04

20. symbol 象徵（名詞）

例句：He sent her a gift as a symbol of his love.

中譯：他寄給她一個象徵愛情的禮物。

21. opportunity 機會（名詞）

例句：You will have an opportunity to ask questions after the break.

中譯：休息過後你會有機會提問。

22. station 站（名詞）

例句：The bus station was straight across the street from his office.

中譯：這個巴士站在他辦公室的正對面。

station 駐守（動詞）

例句：The soldiers will be stationed at this base for one year.

中譯：這批軍人會在這個基地駐守一年。

23. task 工作、任務（名詞）

例句：Every morning I make a list of tasks I want to achieve that day.

中譯：每天早上我會開一張當天要完成任務的清單。

24. independent 獨立（形容詞）

例句：He moved out of his parents' house because he wanted to be independent.

中譯：他搬離父母家，因為他想獨立。

 independence 獨立（名詞）

例句：This small country just announced its independence.

中譯：這個小國剛宣布獨立。

25. serious 嚴肅的（形容詞）

例句：The doctor is known to be very serious and rarely smiles.

中譯：眾所周知，這位醫生非常嚴肅、鮮少有笑容。

26. former 以前的（形容詞）

例句：I am still in contact with my former boss from my first job.

中譯：我跟我以前第一個工作的老闆還保持聯絡。

III. Introducing Yourself at a Conference （Email Version）
研習會自我介紹（電子郵件篇）

Yasmin 代表華東銀行參加一個研討會，開會之前他先寄了一個自我介紹的電子郵件給與會人士：

🎧 05

Dear fellow conference attendees,

My name is Yasmin Yeoh and I work for Hua Tung Bank in Taipei, Taiwan. I am **extremely** pleased to be **moderating** the policy **committee** at this week's conference.

My **expertise** is mainly in personal **wealth**, but I have a **broad range** of interests in both local and **global** business. I hope I can **explore** these areas with all of you over the next five days.

If anyone is interested in getting together after regular conference hours to **exchange** more ideas and information, please email me at Yasmin@htbank. com.tw.

I look forward to sharing a wonderful conference together with you.

Best regards,
Yasmin Yeoh

▌中譯

各位參加研習會的學員，您好，

我的名字叫做 Yasmin Yeoh，我在台北華東銀行工作，非常高興能為本星期會議中主持政策委員會。

我的專長是經管個人財務，但我的興趣廣泛，志在本地及全球業務，我希望在接下

來的五天裡可以在這些方面與各位砌磋。

如果各位有興趣在會後交換意見和資訊，請寫信到以下的地址：
Yasmin@htbank.com.tw

期待與您們共享一個美好的研討會！

Yasmin Yeoh 敬上

 06

27. extreme 極端的、激烈的（形容詞）

例句：He thought his father's political views were too extreme.

中譯：他認為他的父親的政治主張太過激烈。

> 延伸　**extremely** 極端地，非常地（副詞）
>
> 例句：She was extremely thankful to the rescuers who saved her life.
>
> 中譯：她非常感謝救難者救了她一命。

28. moderate 協調（討論會）（動詞）

例句：The person who moderates a debate must be fair and balanced.

中譯：擔任辯論仲裁的人應該是公平，不偏不倚的。

moderate 中庸的、適度的、穩健的（形容詞）

例句：He had very moderate political opinions; he wasn't too far left or too far right.

中譯：他的政治觀點中庸：不偏左也不偏右。

29. committee 委員會（名詞）

例句：All the committee members supported this project.

中譯：所有的委員會成員都支持這項計畫案。

30. expert 專家（名詞）

例句：The professor is an expert on global warming research.

中譯：這位教授是全球暖化的研究專家。

> **expertise** 專長
>
> 例句：The professor's expertise is in global warming research.
>
> 中譯：這位教授的專長在做全球暖化的研究。

31. wealth 財富（名詞）

例句：He earned his wealth through the stock market.

中譯：他從股票市場賺取財富。

> **wealthy** 有錢的
>
> 例句：Although he is extremely wealthy, this man has serious depression problems.
>
> 中譯：雖然很富有，這位人士卻有嚴重的憂鬱症。

32. broad 寬廣的（形容詞）

例句：They built a huge house on a broad piece of land.

中譯：他們在一片寬廣的土地上蓋了巨宅。

33. range 範圍（名詞）

例句：The age range of employees in the company is 22 to 62.

中譯：這家公司員工的年齡層是 22 到 62 歲。

range 介於……範圍之間（動詞）

例句：Their ages range from 22 to 62.

中譯：他們的年齡介於 22 到 62 歲。

34. global 全球的（形容詞）

例句：We are a global company. We have offices on six continents.

中譯：我們是一家全球化的公司，我們在六大洲都有分公司。

 延伸　**globalize** 使全球化（動詞）

例句：Your firm is too local; you need to globalize your business.

中譯：你的公司太本土，你應該將業務全球化。

globalization 全球化（名詞）

例句：The age of globalization is coming. We had better be prepared.

中譯：全球化時代來臨了，我們最好做好準備。

35. explore 探索（動詞）

例句：Traveling lets me explore different cultures and traditions.

中譯：旅行讓我能探索不同的文化和傳統。

36. exchange 交換（名詞）

例句：The exchange rate for the US dollar has decreased this year.

中譯：今年美金兌換率已經跌了。

exchange 交換（動詞）

例句：We exchanged email addresses and phone numbers at the party.

中譯：我們在派對上交換了電子郵件地址和電話號碼。

IV. Introducing Yourself at a Conference （Oral Presentation）

會議自我介紹（口語篇）

在大會一開始，與會人士一一自我介紹，請看口語的自我介紹與書寫式的有何不同：

Hello everyone,

My name is Yasmin Yeoh. You can call me Yasmin. I work for Hua Tung Bank in Taipei, Taiwan. I am happy to attend this week's conference.

My expertise is mainly in personal wealth, but I am also interested in local and global business. I look forward to discussing and sharing ideas with you in all of these areas over the next five days.

Thank you.

中譯

各位好，

我的名字是 Yasmin Yeoh。你們可以就叫我 Yasmin。我在台灣台北華東銀行工作，很高興能參加這個會議。

我的專長主要是經管私人財務，而我對本地和全球業務也都有接觸。我期待在未來五天裡能跟各位在這些方面多多交流。

謝謝。

V. Introducing Yourself at a Conference Party (Dialogue Version)

會議自我介紹（會話篇）

會議歡迎晚宴上，代表 123 國際公司的 Nate 與代表華東銀行的 Yasmin 相遇，他們各自自我介紹後聊了起來：

🎧 08

> Nate: Hi there! Nate Stein from 123 International.
> Yasmin: Nice to meet you, Mr. Stein. My name's Yasmin Yeoh. I represent Hua Tung Bank.
> Nate: Good to meet you, and please just call me Nate. Where are you from?
> Yasmin: Taipei, Taiwan.
> Nate: Wow, you've traveled a long way to get here. What brings you to this conference?
> Yasmin: I'm moderating the policy committee this week. How about you?
> Nate: I'm a banker from New York City. I was thinking about attending your committee. What types of **issues** are you thinking of **covering**?
> Yasmin: The committee will **be based on** my expertise in **private** wealth and finance, but I'm also really interested in global business trade.
> Nate: I may not have time to go to your committee, but we should talk more after the conference. Here's my business card. Get in touch.
> Yasmin: Great, thanks Nate. I'll give you a call.

中譯

Nate：嗨，我是 123 國際公司的 Nate Stein。

Yasmin：幸會，Stein 先生，我的名字是 Yasmin Yeoh，我代表華東銀行。

Nate：幸會，請叫我 Nate。你是哪裡人？

Yasmin：我從台灣的台北來的。

Nate：哇！你從大老遠飛到這裡。請問您此行的目的是什麼？

Yasmin：這星期由我主持政策委員會，你呢？

Nate：我在紐約市的銀行服務，我正在想要不要參加你們的委員會，請問你們打
算涵蓋哪些類型的議題呢？

Yasmin：我們的委員會是以我私人理財方面的專長為主，但我對全球貿易也很有興趣。

Nate：我也許沒時間參加你主持的委員會，但我們可以在會後多聊聊。這是我的
名片，再聯絡。

Yasmin：太好了，Nate，謝謝，我會打電話給你。

 09

37. issue 議題（名詞）

例句：The way he treats female workers in the office has become a big issue.

中譯：他對待辦公室女性員工的態度引發爭議。

issue 發佈（動詞）

例句：The company issued a press release today about their newest product.

中譯：這家公司發布新聞，介紹他們的新產品。

38. cover 涵蓋（動詞）

例句：This meeting will cover many important issues.

中譯：這次會議將涵蓋許多重要的議題。

cover 封面（名詞）

例句：The book covers she designed are all very attractive.

中譯：她設計的書封都很吸引人。

39. base 基礎、基地（名詞）

例句：He used Taichung as a base for his global business.

中譯：他用台中當作他全球業務的基地。

based on 基於、根據

例句：Based on the committee's decision, we shouldn't contact them first.

中譯：基於委員會的決議，我們不能先跟他們接觸。

40. private 私人的、注重隱私的（形容詞）

例句：He is a very private person and doesn't like sharing his thoughts in public.

中譯：他是位很重隱私的人，不會在公共場合跟人說他的想法。

---

 privacy 隱私

例句：To protect his own privacy, he never shows his family photos to other people.

中譯：為保護他的隱私，他從不把家人的照片秀給別人看。

in private 私下

例句：I don't understand why she would rather talk with me in private.

中譯：我不瞭解為什麼她寧願跟我私下談。

I. Multiple Choice 選擇題

1. (　) As soon as she settled in, she started to _____ the new city she had just moved to.

   (a) moderate (b) welcome (c) explore

2. (　) Her _____ is training new teachers.

   (a) expert (b) expertise (c) branch

3. (　) How long have you been working in the Taipei _____ of the bank?

   (a) joint (b) branch (c) task

4. (　) Do you know the meanings of those common signs and _____?

   (a) ranges (b) majors (c) symbols

5. (　) I took the old bottles to the store to _____ them for money.

   (a) exchange (b) responsibility (c) private

6. (　) The _____ party leader is in jail right now.

   (a) symbol (b) broad (c) former （party leader 黨主席，in jail 坐牢）

7. (　) She is the chairperson of the _____.

   (a) broad (b) board (c) politics

8. (　) He is responsible for this major _____.

   (a) speed (b) symbol (c) task

9. (　) May I talk with this business in _____ ?

   (a) opportunity (b) private (c) branch

10. (　) There will be a broad _____ of opportunities in front of you in the near future.

    (a) range (b) support (c) station

II. Fill in the Blank 請選適當的字填入空格中，沒有用到的字請劃掉

> expert, supervise, former, represent, private

Jonathan Shaw 寫信給 Mr. Smith，信中介紹代表他自己公司與 Smith 的公司接洽生意的資深業務代表 Samuel Pan：

Dear Mr. Smith,

I would like to introduce you to Samuel Pan. Samuel is our company's top 1._____ on export finance（出口業務）and was a(n) 2._____ advisor to the president.

Because of his expertise, I have asked him to 3._____ your latest business deal. He will contact your office in the next couple of days to arrange a(n) 4._____ meeting with you.

As always, please feel free to contact me if you have any questions or concerns.

Kind regards,
Jonathan Shaw

III. Fill in the Blank 請選適當的字填入空格中，沒有用到的字請劃掉

> politics, completed, major, serious, opportunity

Josh 在會議前自我介紹，談他個人的專業、嗜好及個性：

Hi everyone,

My name is Josh Tsai and I will be attending this weekend's conference.
I just 1. _____ my degree at the National Taiwan Normal University.
Though my 2. _____ in college was in science, I also enjoy discussing other
subjects like sports, rock music, and 3._____ with my friends.

I'm really looking forward to debating various issues with all of you at the
conference -- even though I'm usually a very laid back person and don't like to
be too 4. _____ about anything. (laid back 悠閒、自在、懶散的)

See you all this weekend,
Josh

🔒 **A**nswer Key 解答

I. Multiple Choice

1	2	3	4	5	6	7	8	9	10
c	b	b	c	a	c	b	c	b	a

II. Fill in the Blank

1	2	3	4
expert	former	supervise	private

III. Fill in the Blank

1	2	3	4
completed	major	politics	serious

Chapter 2

Making Contact
建立關係

剛進社會的新鮮人，第一步需要學習的是如何
建立人際關係。本章教你如何用簡單明瞭的
Globish 單字，寫信或打電話聯絡客戶、以拓
展業務。

I. Formal Contact（Email Version）
正式聯絡客戶（電子郵件篇）

林伯堅先生是 **ABC** 公司的業務代表，他用電子郵件第一次聯絡客戶 **Smith** 先生，
同時信中介紹一套 **ABC** 公司新推出的刀具：

🎧 10

Dear Mr. Smith,

My name is Bo Jian Lin and I represent ABC Company. I want to **inform** you
about our newly **released set** of high-**quality** kitchen knives.

I have **attached** some photos and **product** information with this email to
show you all of the kitchen knives **available**. If you have any **questions** or
would like to get a price **estimate**, please **contact** me at my office.

Thank you for your **attention**.

Bo Jian Lin
Sales Representative, ABC Company,
Cell: 0937-123-456
bojian.lin@email.com

中譯

Smith 先生，您好，

我的名字是林伯堅，代表 ABC 公司。我想告知您有關我們新推出的高級廚房刀具
的消息。

在這封電子郵件的附件裡，您可以看到我們所有刀具產品的圖片和資料，如果您有
任何問題，或需要我們提供報價，請跟我聯絡。

謝謝。

林伯堅
ABC 公司業務代表
手機：0937-123-456
bojian.lin@email.com

⌒11

1. inform 通知、告知（動詞）

例句：I will inform you when the chairperson is ready to see you.

中譯：主席可以見您時，我會通知您。

 information 資訊，情報（名詞）

例句：The customer wanted more information about the
product before buying it.

中譯：顧客購買產品前，想知道這個產品更多的資訊。

2. release 發佈、推出（動詞）

例句：Every quarter, the company releases a profit report.

中譯：每一季公司都會發布盈利報告。

 newly released 剛發佈的（形容詞）

例句：I'm really interested in reading the government's
newly released report.

中譯：我很有興趣讀政府剛發布的報告。

3. set 安排（動詞）（動詞三態變化都一樣）set, set, set

例句：Have you set the date for our meeting?

中譯：你安排好我們見面（開會）的日期嗎？

例句：I will order a set lunch.

中譯：我會點午餐定食。

set 組合、一套（名詞）

例句：I just bought a set of teacups for my sister.

中譯：我剛買了一套茶杯給我姊姊。

4. quality 質量、品質（名詞）

例句：We refuse to accept bad-quality products.

中譯：我們拒絕接受品質不良的產品。

 high-quality 高規格、優質的（形容詞）

例句：We make the best products because we only use high-quality materials.

中譯：我們製造最好的產品因為我們只用高規格的原料。

5. attach 附加（動詞）

例句：I attached a document to this email.

中譯：隨這封電子郵件我附加了一份文件。

 attachment 附件、副件、附加檔案（名詞）

例句：My photo is in the attachment.

中譯：我的照片在附加檔案中。

6. product 產品（名詞）重音在前 pro

例句：We sell our products on the market for a fair price.

中譯：我們在市場上用公道的價錢賣我們的產品。

 produce 製造、生產（動詞）重音在後 duce

例句：Our company produces everything at a factory in Taiwan.

中譯：我們公司的每樣東西都在台灣的工廠生產。

7. available 有供應的 （形容詞）

例句：The Apple Store will not have any iPads available until next summer.

中譯：這家蘋果專賣店要到明年夏天才會供應 iPad。

8. comment 評語、指教（名詞）重音在前 com

例句：Customers can leave comments about the new knives on our website.

中譯：顧客可以在我們網站留言指教我們的新刀具。

comment 點評、議論（動詞）重音在後 ment

例句：Customers have commented about the new knives on our website.

中譯：顧客們已在我們的網站上點評了新刀具。

9. question 詢問、問題（名詞）

例句：Customers can also send us questions by mail.

中譯：顧客可以用郵件寄給我們詢問（有關產品的問題）。

question 詢問、質疑（動詞）

例句：He is questioning my future plan for the company.

中譯：他質疑我對公司未來的規劃。

10. estimate 報價、估價（名詞）

例句：Can you give me an estimate for replacing all the broken chairs?

中譯：你可以給我汰換所有壞掉的椅子的報價嗎？

estimate 估算（動詞）

例句：How much do you estimate this program will cost?

中譯：你估算這個計畫要花多少錢？

11. contact 聯絡、接觸（名詞）

例句：I finally made contact with this officer yesterday.

中譯：我昨天終於跟這位官員聯絡上了。

contact 聯絡（動詞）

例句：Please contact me as soon as possible.

中譯：請儘快跟我聯絡。

12. attention 注意（名詞）

例句：Our employees will pay attention to every detail.

中譯：我們的員工會注意每一個細節。

II. Making Business Contacts（Telephone Version）
聯絡客戶（電話篇）

ABC 公司的業務員林伯堅打電話給梅花牌廚具店採購主任 Mary，向她推銷刀具：

🎧 12

Mary: Hello, The Meihua Kitchen Store, this is Mary speaking.

Bo Jian: Hi Mary. My name is Bo Jian Lin, I am a sales representative from ABC Company. May I please speak with the person **in charge of** purchasing for your store?

Mary: That's me. I am the **head** of the **purchasing division**.

Bo Jian: Great. Mary, as I said, I am from ABC Company and we have just released a new set of kitchen knives. They are made of high-quality **metals**, light **weight**, and low cost. You will not find anything else like them on the **market** right now.

Mary: That's very interesting. We are looking for new products to bring into the store. Can you send me more **details**?

Bo Jian: Of course! I have **pictures** and information on all the knives. What is the best way to send them to you?

Mary: Just email them to me. My email is mary@thekitchenstore.com.tw.

Bo Jian: I will email you the information right away and **follow up** again at the end of week. If you have any questions before then, my contact information will be in the email. Feel free to contact me any time.

Mary: Sounds good.

Bo Jian: Thanks for your time, Mary. I'll talk to you again on Friday.

中譯

Mary：喂，這裡是梅花廚具店，我是 Mary。

伯堅：嗨，Mary，我的名字是林伯堅，我是 ABC 公司的業務員。我可不可以跟你們店裡負責採購的人員講話？

Mary：我就是採購部門的負責人。

伯堅：太好了，Mary，我剛說過，我是 ABC 公司的業務員，我們剛出了一系列廚房刀具，是由高品質的金屬打造、輕巧、低價位，現在市面上還看不到跟我們同等級的產品。

Mary：很有意思，我們店裡正在找新產品，你可以寄一些詳細的資料給我嗎？

伯堅：當然可以，我有所有刀具的照片和資料。請問用什麼方式寄給您最好？

Mary：用電子郵件就可以了，我的電子郵箱是：mary@thekitchenstore.com.tw。

伯堅：我會馬上用電子郵件把資料寄給您，週末前我會做後續工作。如果在這之前你有何問題，我聯絡方法都在電子郵件裡，請不要客氣，隨時跟我聯絡。

Mary：聽起來不錯。

伯堅：Mary，謝謝您寶貴的時間，星期五我會再跟您聯絡。

 13

13. charge 費用（名詞）

例句：There is a NT$ 50 charge to enter the park.

中譯：進公園要收 50 元新台幣的費用。

charge 收費、要價（動詞）

例句：This store charges less than the one by my office.

中譯：這家店收費比我辦公室旁邊的那家少。

 in charge 主持，主掌

例句：When my boss is away, I am in charge of the office.

中譯：老闆不在時由我主掌辦公室。

14. head 首腦、主管（名詞）

例句：You need to ask the head of the division; she is in charge.

中譯：你得問這部門的主管，是她在主其事。

head 領導（動詞）

例句：She will head a team of researchers on this project.

中譯：她會領導一組研究員做這個專案。

15. **purchase** 購買（名詞）

例句：For that price, it was a good purchase.

中譯：用那樣的價位，算得上是好採購。

purchase 購買（動詞）

例句：We don't have enough money to purchase this property.

中譯：我沒有足夠的錢買這個房產。

---

 purchasing department 採購部

例句：We are out of supplies; please ask the purchasing department to send out a new order.

中譯：我們的供貨不足了，請叫採購部門開出新的採購單。

---

16. **divide** 分組（動詞）

例句：The group is too large; let's divide it into three smaller teams.

中譯：這個團體太大了，讓我們把它分成三個小組。

---

 division 部門（名詞）

例句：His boss moved him to a different division of the company.

中譯：他老闆把它調到公司不同的部門。

---

17. **metal** 金屬（名詞）

例句：Metals like gold and silver are very expensive.

中譯：像金或銀之類的金屬很貴。

18. **weight** 重量（名詞）

例句：He has successfully lost some weight.

中譯：他減重成功。

weigh 秤重（動詞）

例句：How much do you weigh? I weigh 65kg.

中譯：你多重？我 65 公斤重。

19. market 市場（名詞）

例句：The housing market has been very slow all year.

中譯：整年的房屋市場都不景氣。

market 推銷（動詞）

例句：To get a job, you need to know how to market yourself to companies.

中譯：要找到工作，你需要知道如何把自己推銷給公司。

20. detail 細節（名詞）

例句：He inspected the item closely so he could see if there were any problems in the details.

中譯：他仔細檢查這件東西，以便看出細節裡是否有毛病。

 detailed 詳細的（形容詞）

例句：I made a detailed list for you to follow.

中譯：我開了一張詳細的清單讓你照著做。

21. picture 圖片、照片（名詞）

例句：His new camera takes great pictures.

中譯：他新的相機照出很棒的相片。

picture 想像（動詞）

例句：I can't picture myself working for any other company.

中譯：我無法想像自己能為其他任何公司工作。

22. follow 追隨、聽從（動詞）

例句：She didn't follow her supervisor's suggestions.

中譯：她沒有聽從主管（或指導教授）的建議。

延伸　**follow up** 做後續工作、收尾（動詞）

例句：I followed up the email with a phone call to her office.

中譯：寫了電子郵件後，我再打了一通電話到她辦公室。

follow-up 後續行動（名詞）

例句：The shop accepted my complaint, but there wasn't any follow-up.

中譯：這家店接受我的抱怨，但卻沒有任何後續動作。

III. Informal Contact（Email Version）
用非正式的聯絡（電子郵件篇）

素珊在公司會計部門工作，她想私下約另一個部門的同事 John 商談辦公室的業務：

 14

Hi John,

It's Su-shan from the **accounting** office. I just **received** your **report** on Tuesday.

I had some **concerns** about the **current** budget of our **advertisement** **campaign**. Can we meet up for a **meal** later this week to **discuss**?

Talk soon,
Su-shan

中譯

嗨，John，

我是會計部門的素珊，星期二剛收到你的報告。

我對公司本季廣告的預算有些疑慮，這禮拜吃個飯談一談好嗎？

之後再聊，
素珊

23. account 帳目、戶頭、客戶（名詞）

例句：Our account has lost a large amount of money this year.

中譯：今年我們帳目裡損失了一大筆錢。

例句：He withdrew some money from his bank account.

中譯：他從他的戶頭裡提領了一些錢。

例句：Our company has three major accounts.

中譯：我們公司有三個主要的客戶。

> **accounting** 會計（名詞）
>
> 例句：His major in college was accounting.
>
> 中譯：他在大學的主修是會計。
>
> **accountant** 會計師（名詞）
>
> 例句：My accountant helps me with all my finances.
>
> 中譯：我的會計師幫我管財務。

24. receive 收到（動詞）

例句：We receive thousands of emails every day asking about our products.

中譯：我每天收到好幾千封的電子郵件，詢問我們公司的產品。

> **receptionist** 接待員（名詞）
>
> 例句：The receptionist welcomed the group at the door.
>
> 中譯：接待員在門口歡迎來訪的團體。

25. report 報告（動詞）

例句：As soon as you receive any information, immediately report it to me.

中譯：當你接到任何消息，立刻向我報告。

report 報告（名詞）

例句：We have to write a report about the election.

中譯：我們必須寫一份有關選舉的報告。

26. concern 考量、關注（名詞）

例句：Succeeding in the global market is my main concern.

中譯：在全球市場成功是我主要的考量。

 be concerned about 關注、擔心（動詞）

例句：There's no need to be concerned about the amount of money we spend.

中譯：不需要擔心我們要花少錢。

27. current 目前的（形容詞）

例句：Young people today pay little attention to current events.

中譯：現在的年輕人很少注意時事。

 currently 目前（副詞）

例句：My boss is currently on holiday, but he'll be back next week.

中譯：我老闆目前在度假，但他下星期會回來。

28. advertisement 廣告（名詞）

例句：Print and broadcast advertisements are the best way to appeal to the public.

中譯：印刷或電子媒體的廣告是最好吸引大眾的方式。

advertising 宣傳、打廣告的（形容詞）

例句：The advertising agency is famous for designing campaign signs.

中譯：這家廣告公司以設計促銷活動的看板出名。

advertise 宣傳、打廣告（動詞）

例句：They advertised the product in the local paper.

中譯：他們在當地報紙上為產品打廣告。

29. campaign 有競爭性質的活動，如競選、促銷活動（名詞）

例句：We are starting a campaign to raise money for the new school.

中譯：我們為建新學校展開了的募款活動。

campaign 競選（動詞）

例句：He campaigned for Parliament last year, but did not win.

中譯：他去年競選國會議員，但沒選上。

30. meal 餐飲（名詞）

例句：Dinner is my favorite meal of the day.

中譯：晚餐是一天中我最喜歡的一餐。

31. discuss 討論（動詞）

例句：We will discuss the community's environmental issues with our boss.

中譯：我們要跟老闆討論社區環保的議題。

 discussion 討論（名詞）

例句：We need to have a discussion about our marketing campaigns.

中譯：我們需要討論一下市場的促銷活動。

I. Multiple Choice 選擇題

1. (　) Please _____ us if you receive any interesting information about their new product.

　　(a) discuss　(b) release　(c) inform

2. (　) Have you read the card _____ to the flowers?

　　(a) attached (b) released (c) designed

3. (　) How much money do you still have in your _____ ?

　　(a) concern (b) quality (c) account

4. (　) She is _____ the quality of our products.

　　(a) concerning　(b) questioning (c) purchasing

5. (　) They just _____ a piece of news about the campaign.

　　(a) released　(b) contacted　(c) met

6. (　) Who will _____ our company and attend the meeting?

　　(a) receive　(b) represent　(c) comment

7. (　) There are lots of public _____ about the newly released advertisement.

　　(a) qualities　(b) concerns　(c) products

8. (　) I don't like the _____ advertisement for our product. I think the one we had before is better.

　　(a) estimated　(b) high-quality　(c) current

9.(　) When do you have time to _____ the current community environmental issues with us?

　　(a) comment　(b) discuss　(c) question

10. (　) Please pay _____ to her boss's comments on our design.

　　(a) account　(b) contact　(c) attention

II. Fill in the Blank 請選適當的字填入空格中，沒有用到的字請劃掉

attention, comment, quality, receive, release, represent

Vivian 寫信給 Mr. Jones，告知她們的公司已收到 Mr. Jones 公司寄來產品改良的意見，並表示公司一定會正視他給的寶貴意見：

Dear Mr. Jones,

My name is Vivian Wu. Currently, I 1._____Minyao Industries' public relations department（公關部門）.

Thank you for sending us your 2._____s about our product. Our company pays close 3._____ to every message we 4._____. We will inform you when we 5._____more news.

Thank you again for your patience and continued support.

Sincerely,

Vivian

III. Fill in the Blank 請選適當的字填入空格中，沒有用到的字請劃掉

> meal, advertisement, concernl, discuss, contact

Jenn 和 Pete 是公司同事。Pete 寫短信邀約在不同部門工作的 Jenn 吃午餐，順便討論一下公司內部的業務：

Hi Jenn,

This is Pete from the Customer Service division. Are you free tomorrow to meet
and 1._____ some of the 2. _____s we've received about the current
3._____s? Let's go for a 4._____ and talk about it.

Let me know,
Pete

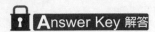

Answer Key 解答

I. Multiple Choice

1	2	3	4	5	6	7	8	9	10
c	a	c	b	a	b	b	c	b	c

II. Fill in the Blank

1	2	3	4	5
represent	comment	attention	receive	release

III. Fill in the Blank

1	2	3	4
discuss	concern	advertisement	meal

Chapter 3

Asking for
Information / Help
要求提供資訊或懇請協助

建立人際關係之後，需要開始收集資訊和情報。
資訊和情報並非唾手可得，需要靠勤寫信和勤打
電話。其實用簡單的 **Globish** 單字，就能敲開
大門，取得你所需。

I. Formal Request（Email Version）
正式的請求（電子郵件篇）

華東銀行的李民生先生希望有機會跟劉美惠任職的貿易公司合作，但想請劉小姐先寄一些公司資料給他：

🎧 16

Dear Ms. Mei Hui Liu,

I represent a large banking **firm**, Hua Tung. Our bank is **seeking investment** opportunities to help customers grow. We are **especially interested** in an **international import** and **export** company. Our **research indicates** that your company might be a good **fit** for us, but we would like to learn more about your current **financial status**.

Could you please send us a copy of your most up to date financial report, including the **budget** for this year? Please also include a list of your **projected costs** and **returns**.

I look forward to hearing from you.

Sincerely,
Min-sheng Li
Account Executive,
HuaTung Investment Bank

中譯

劉美惠女士，您好，

我代表一家名叫華東的開發銀行。現在我們正尋求投資機會與顧客共創商機。我們特別有興趣的合作對象是國際進出口公司。據我們的研究顯示，貴公司正屬於我們的上選，但我們想知道更多關於你們目前的財務狀況。

可否請貴公司寄一份最近的財務報告，包括今年的預算、預估的成本和收益清單。

我們期待您的回音。

李民生敬上
會計主任
華東開發銀行

Globish
單字

🎧 17

1. firm 公司、事務所（名詞）

例句：Lisa was hired by a legal firm straight out of school.

中譯：麗莎剛出校門就被一家律師事務所聘用了。

firm 穩定的（形容詞）

例句：Taiwan dollars stay firm against American dollars.

中譯：台幣兌美金匯率保持穩定。

2. seek 尋找、徵求（動詞）（動詞三態 seek, sought, sought）

例句：You should seek advice from an expert.

中譯：你應該徵求專家的意見。

3. invest 投資（動詞）

例句：He decided to invest his money in the stock market instead of saving it in the bank.

中譯：他決定投資股票市場，不存在銀行裡。

 延伸 **investment** 投資（名詞）

例句：Taiwan wants to attract more foreign investment.

中譯：台灣想吸引更多的外國投資。

investor 投資者 / 投資公司（名詞）

例句：An investor is a person or an organization that invests money.

中譯：Investor 指的是投資錢的人或組織。

4. **especially** 特別地（副詞）

例句：The market is especially weak right now.

中譯：市場目前特別地疲軟。

5. **interest** 興趣（名詞）

例句：He has no interest in science.

中譯：他對科學沒有興趣。

interest 利息（名詞）

例句：What is the interest rate for a savings account?

中譯：活期存款戶頭的利率是多少？

---

 be interested in 有興趣

例句：I am interested in Finland's educational system.

中譯：我對芬蘭的教育體制很有興趣。

interesting 有趣的（形容詞）

例句：This experimental project is very interesting.

中譯：這個實驗性的工作計畫真有趣。

---

6. **international** 國際的（形容詞）

例句：The two countries just signed an international trade agreement.

中譯：這兩個國家剛簽訂了一項國際貿易協定。

7. **import** 進口（動詞）

例句：Canada must import lots of fruits and vegetables because it is too cold to grow them there.

中譯：加拿大得進口很多水果和蔬菜，因為當地太冷無法種植蔬果。

import 進口（名詞）

例句：Imports of certain items are forbidden.

中譯：某些東西的進口是不允許的。

imported 進口的（形容詞）

例句：Imported goods are often more expensive than local goods.

中譯：進口的東西通常比在地的產品貴。

8. export 出口（動詞）

例句：China exports more goods than any other country in the world.

中譯：中國比世界上任何其他國家出口更多的產品。

export 進口（名詞）

例句：Japan's exports have started to grow more slowly.

中譯：日本出口的成長開始放慢。

 exported 出口的

例句：All the exported apples have been rejected.

中譯：所有出口的蘋果都被退貨。

9. research 研究（名詞）

例句：Part of his research includes doing science experiments in the laboratory.

中譯：他部分的研究工作包括在實驗室裡做科學實驗。

research 研究（動詞）

例句：We are researching the effects of smoking on dogs and cats.

中譯：我們正在研究抽煙對狗和貓的影響。

10. indicate 指出、顯示（動詞）

例句：Red flashing lights indicate that it is not safe to drive.

中譯：閃紅燈表示開車不安全。

11. fit 適合（動詞）

例句：The jacket fits him just right.

中譯：這件夾克的大小對他正合適。

fit 適合的（形容詞）

例句：He is not really fit for this job.

中譯：他並不適合做這個工作。

> **good fit** 正合適（名詞）
>
> 例句：His obedient character was a good fit for the military.
>
> 中譯：他順服的個性正適合軍旅生活。

12. finance 財務、金融、財源周轉（名詞）

例句：Parents have to teach their children how to handle their finances.

中譯：父母應該教子女如何理財。

finance 資助（動詞）

例句：My parents agreed to finance my college education.

中譯：我父母答應了資助我的大學教育。

> **financial** 財務的（形容詞）
>
> 例句：Our company will offer all kinds of financial services.
>
> 中譯：我們公司將提供各種財務管理的業務服務。

13. status 狀況（名詞）

例句：We are concerned about the current political status of your country.

中譯：我們關心你國家目前的政治狀況。

social status 社會地位

例句：In many Asian countries, a teacher's social status is very high.

中譯：在許多亞洲國家，老師的社會地位很高。

marital status 婚姻狀況

例句：She wrote "single" in the blank space under "Marital Status."

中譯：她在「婚姻狀況」欄填上「單身」。

14. budget 財務預算（名詞）

例句：My boss is trying to balance our company's budget.

中譯：我的老闆正努力去平衡公司的財務預算。

15. project 計畫、工程項目（名詞）（重音在第一音節 pro）

例句：Building a road through the mountains is a big project.

中譯：開造一條穿過群山的路是一項大工程。

project 設想、籌劃（動詞）（重音在第二音節 ject）

例句：The embassy projected the two countries' future development.

中譯：大使館籌劃出兩國未來的發展。

 projector 投影機

例句：She is using a projector to show us the chart of birth rates from 2000 to 2011.

中譯：她用投影機顯示從 2000 年到 2011 年的出生率圖表。

16. cost 花費、開銷（名詞）

例句：The cost of living in Taipei is increasing.

中譯：台北的生活費愈來愈高。

cost 花（動詞）（動詞三態變化）cost, cost, cost

例句：It cost me 1000 NT to buy fuel for my car.

中譯：我花了台幣 1000 元給我的車子加油。

17. return 報酬、利潤（名詞）

例句：This investment does not guarantee a high return.

中譯：這項投資不保證有高報酬。

return 返回（動詞）

例句：The soldiers will return home once the war is over.

中譯：戰爭結束後軍人將返回家園。

延伸 **file the tax return** 報稅

例句：You have to file the tax return by the end of May.

中譯：你必須在五月底之前報稅。

II. Formal Request (Telephone Version)
提出請求（電話篇）

華東銀行的業務員李民生先生打電話給劉美惠小姐，在電話中詢問一起合作投資案的進展情況：

🎧 18

Mei-hui: Hello, this is Mei-hui Liu.

Min-sheng: Hi, Ms. Liu. This is Min-sheng Li from Hua Tung Bank calling. I sent you an email earlier this week about possibly working together on an investment deal. I haven't heard from you yet, so I wanted to call **personally** and follow up with you.

Mei-hui: Oh yes, hi, Mr. Li. I apologize for not writing back earlier.

Min-sheng: That's not a problem. Do you have time right now to discuss the offer?

Mei-hui: Yes, and we are very interested. Hua Tung is such a large bank; we would love to add your **resources** to our company.

Min-sheng: I'm glad to hear you're interested. In my email, I requested a few financial documents, such as your budget and your projected costs and returns. Do you think you will be able to send me those **materials** by next week?

Mei-hui: Yes. I've already contacted our accountants. They should have a report ready for you by Monday morning.

Min-sheng: Great. Thank you so much for your **cooperation**. Do you have any questions for me?

Mei-hui: When can we meet to discuss our business plan?

Min-sheng: Let's review your financial reports first, but I will call you again to set up a face-to-face meeting.

Mei-hui: Sounds good. I'll look forward to your call then.

Min-sheng: Talk to you then. Goodbye.

中譯

美惠：喂，我是劉美惠。

民生：嗨，劉女士，我是華東銀行的李民生。這星期初我寄了一封電子郵件給您，

關於一個我們可能可以合作的投資案，我還沒有接到您的回音，所以我想親自打電話給您，進一步瞭解你們的意向。

美惠：李先生，很抱歉我沒能早些回你的信。

民生：沒問題，您現在有時間討論一下我們的提案？

美惠：有，我們很有興趣。華東是一家規模很大的銀行，我們當然希望加些你們的資產來壯大我們的公司。

民生：很高興知道你們對這個提案有興趣。在我電子郵件中，我請你們提供一些財務報表，例如：預算、預估的成本和收益清單。下星期可以把這些東西寄給我嗎？

美惠：我已經聯絡了我們的會計，他們應該會把這些報表在星期一早上準備好給您。

民生：太好了，謝謝您的合作。還有什麼問題我可以效勞的嗎？

美惠：我們什麼時候才能見面，談我們的投資計畫？

民生：讓我們先審查財務報表過後，不過我會再打電話給您，安排一個面對面的會議。

美惠：很好，我就等您的電話。

民生：再聯絡，再見。

 19

18. person 人（名詞）

例句：My boss is a really good person.

中譯：我的老闆真是一個好人。

 personally 對我個人而言（副詞）

例句：I personally like him, but other people think he is difficult to work with.

中譯：對我本人來講，我蠻喜歡他的，但其他的人認為他很難共事。

personality 個性（名詞）

例句：His strong personality makes him a good leader in the office.

中譯：他果斷的個性使他成為辦公室的優秀領導人。

19. resource 資源、資產（名詞）

例句：Larger companies have the resources to expand their businesses.

中譯：大公司有資源來擴展業務。

20. material 材料（名詞）

例句：I am collecting material for my new book on the history of Taiwan.

中譯：我正在為我有關台灣史的新書收集材料。

21. cooperate 合作、協調（動詞）

例句：These two countries finally decided to stop fighting and to start cooperating.

中譯：這兩個國家終於決定停止爭吵，開始合作。

 延伸　**cooperation** 合作（名詞）

例句：We need everyone's cooperation to improve the environment.

中譯：我們需要每個人的合作來改善環境。

III. Informal Request（Email Version）
非正式的請求（電子郵件篇）

Janet 和 Dave 是同事也是好友，Janet 有要事，想求助於 Dave：

Dave,

I have an **emergency**! I just received an important **request** from our CEO. She wants me to **collect** and **organize** all of our **business records** since last year. You know what else? She **expects** all the **documents** to be ready by tonight. But I'm really busy. Can you **lend** me a hand?

I'd **owe** you one,
Janet

中譯

Dave,

我有個緊急狀況！剛接到執行長重要的要求，她要我收集從去年起的生意往來記錄，你知道還有什麼嗎？她指望我今晚之前準備好所有的文件。但我正忙，想你可以幫個忙吧？

我欠你個人情。
Janet

Globish
單字

 21

22. emergency 緊急狀況（名詞）

例句：He could have died if he hadn't reacted quickly to that fire emergency.

中譯：要不是馬上做了火警的應變，他可能已經死了。

> 延伸　**emergency exit** 緊急出口（名詞）
>
> 例句：She always looks for the emergency exits in the theater before watching the show.
>
> 中譯：她看表演之前總是先找尋劇院的緊急出口。

23. request 要求、請求（名詞）

例句：The bank committee rejected his request for a loan.

中譯：銀行委員會拒絕了他貸款的要求。

request 要求、請求（動詞）

例句：We request that you attend our conference next week.

中譯：我們懇請您參加下週的研討會。

24. collect 收集（動詞）

例句：The government collects taxes on its citizens.

中譯：政府向國民徵稅。

> 延伸　**collection** 收集品、收藏（名詞）
>
> 例句：She has a fine collection of glasses.
>
> 中譯：她玻璃杯的收藏品很精美。

25. organize 整理（動詞）

例句：Let's organize these business letters a little bit.

中譯：讓我們來整理一下這些商業信件。

organization 組織（名詞）

例句：Taiwan has become a member of the World Trade Organization (WTO).

中譯：台灣已成為世界貿易組織的會員。

26. business 商業、生意（名詞）

例句：I am happy to do business with you.

中譯：我很高興跟你做生意。

 Business Class 商務艙

例句：They upgraded us to Business Class.

中譯：他們把我們升等到商務艙。

27. record 紀錄、檔案（名詞）（重音在前，re）

例句：Doctors keep a record of every patient.

中譯：醫生保存有每位病人的紀錄。

record 記錄、錄製（動詞）（重音在後，cord）

例句：They recorded the show. It is not broadcast live.

中譯：他們先錄製好的這段表演。不是現場直播的。

28. expect 以為……當然、指望、期待（動詞）

例句：My mother and father expect me to study hard at school.

中譯：我的爸媽期望我會在學校努力讀書。

 expectation 指望、期望、以為當然的結果（名詞）

例句：I try hard to live up to my parents' expectations.

中譯：我力爭上游以不辜負爸媽對我的期望。

29. document 文件、公文（名詞）

例句：The diplomat refused to sign the document.

中譯：外交官拒絕簽署這分文件。

30. lend 借給（動詞）

例句：He wanted me to lend him money interest free.

中譯：他要我無息借錢給他。

 lend a hand 幫忙

例句：My husband often offers to lend a hand around the house.

中譯：我先生常常在家裡主動幫忙。

31. owe 欠（動詞）

例句：I still owe your sister some money.

中譯：我還欠你姊姊一些錢。

owe you one 欠了你、欠你一個人情

例句：Thanks for helping me last time; I owe you one.

中譯：謝謝你上回幫助我，我欠你一個人情。

I. Multiple Choice 選擇題

1. (   ) I hope our _____ will improve this year.

    (a) document (b) business (c) budget

2. (   ) They will _____ him a hand to pay off the loan for his car.

    (a) lend (b) owe (c) export（pay off the loan 還清貸款）

3. (   ) Her _____ for a permanent job was not successful.

    (a) record (b) return (c) request（permanent job 永久正式的工作）

4. (   ) I still _____ the bank NT$150,000. I won't pay it off until next winter.

    (a) invest (b) project (c) owe

5. (   ) I am looking forward to _____ you soon.

    (a) seeing (b) see (c) seen

6. (   ) If the government refuses to _____ us, our school will be closed.

    (a) finance (b) project (c) invest

7. (   ) He decided to _____ money in the international financial market.

    (a) project (b) cooperate (c) invest

8. (   ) Please write down your name, age, and marital _____.

    (a) document (b) status (c) research

9. (   ) Germany _____ lots of cars each year to other countries.

    (a) indicates (b) seeks (c) exports

10. (   ) They expected a high _____ from exporting silk dresses to
    England.

    (a) return (b) firm (c) finance

II. Fill in the Blank 請選適當的字填入空格中，沒有用到的字請劃掉

> opportunity, export, import, invest, project

Mary 是台灣某食品公司的業務代表，她寫信給在外商公司做事的 Shelly Wen，約時間見面，談談食品進出口的合作事宜：

Dear Ms. Shelly Wen,

My name is Mary Woods. I am a representative from a food company that 1._____s snacks (零食) out of Canada. We are looking for an international firm to help 2._____ our products into Taiwan.

I would like a(n) 3._____ to meet with you in person. I believe this 4._____ could greatly profit both of our organizations.

I look forward to seeing you in the near future.

Sincerely,
Mary

III. Fill in the Blank 請選適當的字填入空格中，沒有用到的字請劃掉

expect, organize, owe, request, record

Mei Rui 寫信給同事 Shelly，請她將這個月在公司的花費單寄給她：

Hey Shelly,

I have a small favor to 1._____. Can you please send me a(n) 2._____ of your expenses from this month? I am trying to 3._____ our finances and figure out how much money we still 4._____ other companies.

Thanks so much,
Mei Rui

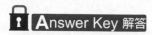
Answer Key 解答

I. Multiple Choice

1	2	3	4	5	6	7	8	9	10
b	a	c	c	a	a	c	b	c	a

II. Fill in the Blank

1	2	3	4
export	import	opportunity	project

III. Fill in the Blank

1	2	3	4
request	record	organize	owe

Chapter 4

Making / Confirming / Changing / Canceling an Appointment
訂定／確認／更改／取消約會

人際關係像一張大網，在這張大網裡，我們約人見面談事情。等約會日期將至，我們會去電提醒對方或再確認約會的時間和地點。但有時因突發的事件，不得不取消先前的約會。這些訂定、確認、更改或取消約會都可以用 Globish 單字來表達。

I. Making a Formal Appointment（Email Version）
訂定正式的約會（電子郵件篇）

Joel Wong 想約時間跟 Anderson 先生見面，談談他的公司團隊將提交給 Anderson 先生的一項新計畫案：

🎧 22

Dear Mr. Anderson,

I **wonder** if you are available next Monday. My **team** has been working hard on the project you gave us last autumn. We have **developed** several ideas and we would like to hear your **opinions** on them.

We will need around 2 hours to **present** our ideas. **However**, I **recognize** this is a very busy time of the year, so please let me know how much time you can give us.

I will follow up with a phone call to your office tomorrow morning. We can organize the **exact** time and place of the meeting then.

Sincerely,
Joel Wong

Anderson 先生，您好，

我想確定您星期一是否有空。我們的團隊已努力完成您去年秋天交付給我們的工作。我們想出了幾個新的點子，並想聽聽您的意見。

我估計需要兩小時來報告我們的計畫，不過我瞭解現在正值一年非常忙碌的時期，請讓我知道您可以勻出多少時間給我們。

明早我會再打一通電話到您的辦公室，我們好敲定會面的確切時間和地點。

Joel Wong 敬上

Globish
單字

23

1. wonder 不知道（因此）想確定（動詞）

例句：I wonder if we can advertise our newly released product in the Sunday paper.

中譯：我想確定我們是否可以在星期天的報紙上為我們新上市產品打廣告。

2. team 團隊、小組（名詞）

例句：A team of researchers will lead the investigation.

中譯：一個研究團隊將主導這項調查。

---

 team player 肯合作的員工

例句：I am sure she will be a great team player in our company.

中譯：我相信她一定會成為公司裡團隊合作的好員工。

team spirit 團隊精神

例句：The group exercises were designed to build team spirit.

中譯：團體體操是為了建立團隊精神而設計的。

---

3. develop 發展、展開（動詞）

例句：The diplomat tried to develop a better relationship with the hostile country.

中譯：外交官員忙著跟有敵意的國家發展出較好的關係。

---

 development 發展（名詞）

例句：The government has released a new land development policy.

中譯：政府已經發布新的土地開發政策。

developed country 發達國家

例句：Developed countries should take more responsibility for helping less developed countries.

中譯：發達國家應負起更多的責任幫助低度開發國家。

developing country 發展中的國家

例句：People in many developing countries lack food and water.

中譯：在許多發展中國家的人民缺水和食物。

4. opinion 意見（名詞）

例句：What is your opinion on the latest government policy?

中譯：你對政府最新的政策有什麼意見？

 opinionated 自以為是的、意見太多的（形容詞）

例句：No one wants to be friends with him because he is too opinionated.

中譯：沒人想跟他做朋友，因為他太自以為是了。

5. present 禮物（名詞）重音在前，pre

例句：The neighbors gave them a present to welcome them to the community.

中譯：鄰居給他們禮物，歡迎他們搬進這個社區。

present 目前的（形容詞）

例句：I'm busy at the present moment. Can you come back later?

中譯：我目前這個時段很忙，你可以待會再來嗎？

present 提交（動詞）重音在後，sent

例句：Investigators will present their evidence to Parliament later this year.

中譯：調查員在後半年會提交證據給國會。

6. however 可是，不過

例句：It's sunny today; however, there may be rain tomorrow.

中譯：今天天氣不錯，不過明天可能會下雨。

7. recognize 認出，發現，瞭解（動詞）

例句：She had changed quite a bit, so it was hard for me to recognize her.

中譯：她變了很多，所以我很難才認出她來。

8. exact 確切的（形容詞）

例句：We haven't set the exact date for the performance yet.

中譯：我們還沒有敲定確切的表演日期。

> **exactly** 確切地（副詞）
>
> 例句：Please tell me exactly what's on your mind.
>
> 中譯：請確切地告訴我你心裡在想什麼。

II. Confirming a Booking（Email Version）
確認預約（電子郵件篇）

Lotus B&B（蓮花民宿）接到顧客 Mandy Wong 的訂房電話後，寫了封電子郵件，確認訂房資訊無誤：

🎧 24

Dear Ms. Mandy Wong,

Thank you for choosing Lotus B&B. We are **pleased** to **confirm** that you have **booked** one **single** room for the nights of May 14 and 15.

The **rate** for each night is NT$ 3,000. This price includes one meal in the morning and parking. Other services, such as **borrowing** bikes or organizing **custom** tours, are also available at an **extra** fee.

If you would like to make any changes to your booking, please feel free to contact us **directly**.

Thank you again and we look forward to seeing you in May,
The Lotus B&B Team

中譯

Mandy Wong 女士，您好，

感謝選擇投宿蓮花民宿，我們很高興跟您確認五月 14、15 日兩晚單人訂房資料。

訂單人房一晚是台幣 3000 元，包括早餐和停車費，我們還提供租腳踏車和安排旅遊，但需另外付費。

如果您需要做任何更改，請直接跟我們聯絡。

再次謝謝，並期待五月與您相見。
蓮花民宿敬上

25

9. please 使高興、使滿意（動詞）

例句：He tried very hard to please the visitors.

中譯：他盡全力讓訪客滿意。

pleased 高興的、滿意的（形容詞）

例句：We're very pleased with your performance so far. Keep up the good work.

中譯：直到目前我們都很滿意你的表現。持續做好工作！

10. confirm 確認（動詞）

例句：He called ahead to confirm their seats at the theater.

中譯：他先打電話確認了他們在劇院的位子。

 confirmation 確認單（名詞）

例句：After booking a room, they received a confirmation from the hotel.

中譯：訂房後，他們接到旅館的確認單。

11. book 書（名詞）

例句：I just started reading a new book.

中譯：我剛開始看一本新書。

book 預訂（動詞）

例句：They booked two train tickets to Kaohsiung.

中譯：他們訂了兩張票去高雄。

 booking 訂房、訂位（名詞）

例句：Sorry, your booking has been canceled.

中譯：對不起，你們的訂位已被取消了。

12. single 單身的、單獨的（形容詞）

例句：I am single. I am not married.

中譯：我是單身，我不是已婚。

例句：I'm used to sleeping by myself in a single bed.

中譯：我習慣一個人睡單人床。

13. rate 價錢、率（名詞）

例句：The rate for a double room is NT$4,000 a night.

中譯：雙人房一晚的價錢是 4000 台幣。

例句：This bank pays the highest interest rate to savers.

中譯：這家銀行付給存戶最高的利率。

例句：Taiwan's birth rate is dropping.

中譯：台灣的出生率下降。

14. borrow 向他人借（動詞）

例句：Can I borrow some cash? I forgot my wallet at home today.

中譯：我可以跟妳借點現金嗎？今天我把皮夾忘在家裡了。

15. custom 習慣、海關（名詞）

例句：It is custom for visitors to bring gifts.

中譯：訪客帶禮物送人是這裡的習慣。

例句：Where should I go to pass through customs?

中譯：我在哪裡通關？

 custom-built, custom-made 為顧客量身打造的（形容詞）

例句：This house is custom-built according to the owner's own designs.

中譯：這棟房子是根據屋主自己的設計量身打造的。

16. extra 額外的（形容詞）

例句：I need an extra week to finish the job.

中譯：我需要多加一個禮拜來完成工作。

17. direct 直接的（形容詞）

例句：If you have a problem, go directly to your boss.

中譯：如果你有問題，直接找你的老闆。

directing 指導、管（動名詞）

例句：He is in charge of directing over 100 employees.

中譯：他負責指揮 100 多名員工。

III. Changing a Booking（Email Version）
改變預約（電子郵件篇）

Mandy Wong 寫電子郵件給蓮花民宿，修改訂房內容：

 26

Dear Lotus B&B,

Last week I booked a single room for the nights of May 14 and 15. However, I was hoping to **extend** my stay. Is it **possible** to change my **departure** date to May 17?

Please let me know if there is room available and what the new cost will be. You can charge my **credit** card for the extra amount. I hope this will not be too much **trouble**.

Many thanks,
Mandy Wong

 中譯

蓮花民宿，

上星期我訂了 5 月 14、15 兩晚單人房，不過我現在希望延長停留時間，可以更改我離開的日期為 5 月 17 日嗎？

請讓我知道有沒有空房，還有新的總價是多少。你可以把多出來的房價算在我的信用卡上。希望沒有為你帶來太多的麻煩。

多謝。
Mandy Wong

Globish
單字

27

18. extend 延長（動詞）

例句：We won't have enough time to finish unless we extend the meeting.

中譯：除非延長開會時間，否則我們沒有足夠的時間開完會。

19. possible 可能的（形容詞）

例句：I am working as fast as possible.

中譯：我正在儘快趕工。

20. departure 離開（名詞）

例句：You need to arrive at the airport at least two hours before departure.

中譯：你必須在起飛兩小時之前到機場。

depart 離開（動詞）

例句：When does your flight depart from Taipei?

中譯：你的飛機幾點從台北起飛？

21. credit 信用（名詞）

例句：Use your credit card for now; we will pay it off later.

中譯：現在先用你的信用卡（付），我們待會再還你錢。

22. trouble 麻煩、問題（名詞）

例句：The company was in a lot of trouble, so it fired its CEO.

中譯：公司出了大問題，所以把執行長給辭退了

trouble 麻煩（動詞）

例句：I'm sorry to trouble you with my problems.

中譯：很抱歉拿我的問題來麻煩你。

IV. Confirming an Appointment
（Telephone Version）
確認約會（電話篇）

Joel 是 Megan 的好友，他打電話給 Megan，以確認他們倆的午餐約會沒改變：

🎧 28

Megan: Hello?

Joel: Hey Megan, it's Joel. I just want to confirm we're still on for lunch today.

Megan: Hi Joel. Yes, I can't wait. I'm **starving** already. Do you have a place in mind?

Joel: I thought we could have a **bite** at the food stand across the street. **According to** my **neighbor**, their fish is the best in town.

Megan: Sounds perfect. What time should we meet?

Joel: I have to return to the office by 2pm for a meeting. Can we meet at the food stand at noon?

Megan: That sounds fine to me.

Joel: Great, see you there, Megan.

中譯

Megan：喂。

Joe：嗨，Megan。我是 Joel。我只是想確認一下今天我們的午餐之約沒變。

Megan：嗨，Joel。對，沒變。我等不及了，早已飢腸轆轆。在什麼地方吃，你心中有譜了嗎？

Joel：我想我們可以先在對街的小吃攤吃，我鄰居說這家的魚是城裡最棒的。

Megan：太好了！我們什麼時候見？

Joel：我下午兩點前得回去開會，我們正午在小吃攤見如何？

Megan：可以。

Joel：好，Megan，小吃攤見。

29

23 starve 飢餓（動詞）

例句：These dogs will starve to death if you don't feed them any food.

中譯：如果你不餵牠們吃點東西，這些狗會餓死。

24 bite 一口（名詞）

例句：He finished that cake in one bite.

中譯：他一口就吃完了那塊蛋糕。

bite 咬（動詞）

例句：When I bite down, my teeth feel loose.

中譯：我咬下去，牙齒覺得鬆動。

> **have a bite** 隨便吃一點
>
> 例句：I'm hungry. Let's go have a bite to eat.
>
> 中譯：我好餓。我們走，去隨便吃點什麼。

25 according to 根據

例句：According to the rules, you are not supposed to swim here.

中譯：根據法令，你不准在這裡游泳。

26 neighbor 鄰居（名詞）

例句：My next door neighbor's apartment is similar to mine.

中譯：我隔壁鄰居的公寓跟我的很相似。

neighborhood 街坊、家的附近地區

例句：There is a camera shop in our neighborhood.

中譯：我們家的附近有家照相器材店。

V. Changing an Appointment （Email Version）
更改正式約會（電子郵件篇）

Anderson 先生無法履行王先生先前之約，請求改期，擇日再會面：

 30

Dear Mr. Wang,

I **regret** I must **postpone** our meeting on Monday because I have been **invited** to **attend** a **conference** next week.

I **apologize** for any trouble this may cause. **Perhaps** we can make another **appointment** for later this month when I have more free time. I am really **looking forward to** hearing about the **progress** you've made on this project.

Best regards,
Kyle Anderson

中譯

王先生，您好，

很遺憾我必須將我們星期一的會面延期，因為下星期我受邀參加一個會議。

很抱歉延期帶來的麻煩，也許我們可以改約在這個月底見，那時候我比較有空。期待聆聽你從事這個計畫案的進展。

Kyle Anderson上

Globish
單字

31

27. regret 後悔、遺憾（動詞）

例句：I regret I didn't get to say goodbye to him before he left the company.

中譯：我後悔在他離開公司之前沒能找機會去跟他道別。

28. postpone 延期（動詞）

例句：The chairman is sick today. Let's postpone this meeting until he feels better.

中譯：老闆今天生病，我們的會議得延期，直到他覺得好些了才能開會。

postponed 被延後（形容詞）

Her trip was postponed because of a family emergency.

因為家庭緊急事故，她的行程被延後。

29. invite 邀約、邀請（動詞）

例句：They invited us to visit a refugee camp.

中譯：他們邀了我們去訪問一個難民營。

 invitation 邀請（名詞）

例句：They turned down our invitation for no reason.

中譯：他們毫無理由的拒絕了我們的邀請。

inviting 誘人的（形容詞）

例句：The water looks inviting, especially on a hot day.

中譯：水看起來真誘人，特別是在大熱天。

30. attend 參加（動詞）

例句：Everyone in the office is required to attend the meeting this afternoon.

中譯：辦公室裡每個人都得參加今天下午的會議。

31. conference 研討會、會議（名詞）

例句：Representatives from all over are attending this conference.

中譯：各地來的代表正在參加這個研討會。

32. apologize 道歉（動詞）

例句：I apologize for making that mistake.

中譯：我為自己犯了那個錯誤道歉。

 apology 道歉（名詞）

例句：I think you owe me an apology.

中譯：我認為你應該跟我道歉。

33. perhaps 或許、大概（副詞）

例句：Perhaps the parcel will be delivered today.

中譯：這個包裹或許今天會送到。

34. appoint 指定、任命（動詞）

例句：She was just appointed the new chairman of the board.

中譯：她被任命當董事會的董事長一職。

 appointment 預約、約會（名詞）

例句：You can't see the doctor unless you have an appointment.

中譯：除非有預約，不然你不能看醫生。

35. look 看（名詞）

例句：When I took a closer look at the product, I found some minor problems.

中譯：當我仔細看了這個產品，我發現一些小問題。

look 看（動詞）

例句：He looked as if he was going to cry.

中譯：他看起來好像要哭的樣子。

> **look forward to +** 動詞 **ing** 期待（信的結尾問候語）
>
> 例句：I look forward to seeing you soon.
>
> 中譯：期待很快可以見到你。

36. progress 進展（名詞）重音在前 pro

例句：Our deal has made great progress; it'll probably be settled soon.

中譯：我們這筆交易大有進展，應該很快就會敲定。

progress 進步、進展（動詞）重音在後 gre

例句：The professor worried his students were not progressing fast enough in their studies.

中譯：教授擔心他的學生在學業上的進步不夠快。

VI. Canceling an Appointment （Telephone Version）
取消普通的約會（電話篇）

May 和 **Brian** 是好友。**May** 突然有急事無法赴約，臨時打電話跟 **Brian** 取消約會：

 32

May: Hi, Brian. It's Mary.

Brian: Hi Mary, how's it going?

May: Not so good. I'm **afraid** (that) I can't make our dinner appointment tonight. I have to **cancel** it.

Brian: Wow, what happened?

May: My dad suddenly became sick this morning. He's in the hospital now and I want to go see him.

Brian: I'm so sorry to hear that. I hope it's nothing serious.

May: Me too, but I don't know much about it yet.

Brian: Is there anything I can do to help?

May: No, but thank you. I'm really sorry for **pulling out** on such short **notice**.

Brian: Don't worry about it. I completely **understand**.

May: Thanks. I'll send you a **message** later.

Brian: Okay, take care.

中譯

May：嗨，Brian, 我是 May。

Brian：嗨，May, 你好嗎？

May：不太好，我恐怕不能赴這禮拜的晚餐約會了。

Brian：哇！怎麼回事？

May：今天早上我爸爸突然病了，我現在得去醫院看他。

Brian：聽到這消息真難過，希望伯父的病不嚴重。

May：但願如此，不過現在我還不知道詳情。

Brian：我可以幫什麼忙嗎？

May：沒事，不過多謝你（的關心），我很抱歉臨時抽身（不能赴約）。
Brian：別擔心，我完全能理解你的處境。
May：謝謝，待會兒我會打電話給你。
Brian：好，自己多保重。

Globish
單字

 33

36. (be) afraid (that)... 恐怕不能、遺憾不能（形容詞）

例句：I am afraid that we won't make it in time to see the movie.

中譯：我恐怕我們無法及時趕上看這場電影。

(be) afraid (of) 害怕

例句：She was afraid of cockroaches and being alone in the dark.

中譯：她怕蟑螂以及在黑暗中獨處。

37. cancel 取消（動詞）

例句：I had to cancel my travel plans when my father was hospitalized.

中譯：爸爸住院時，我得取消我的旅遊計畫。

> **cancellation** 取消、毀約（名詞）
>
> 例句：They will charge you a cancellation fee if you don't show up for your appointment.
>
> 中譯：如果你約了要來卻沒有出現，他們（如旅館）會要你付違約金。

38. pull 抽出（動詞）

例句：He pulled a credit card from his pocket.

中譯：他從口袋抽出一張信用卡。

pull out 抽身、抽腿

例句：They decided to pull out from the car manufacturing business.

中譯：他們決定從汽車製造業抽身而出。

39. notice 注意（動詞）

例句：Have you noticed anything different?

中譯：你注意到有什麼不同嗎？

notice 啓事、通知、佈告（名詞）

例句：Did you read the notice on the door?

中譯：你讀了門上的啓事沒有？

 short notice 臨時通知、倉促通知

例句：He called the meeting on such short notice that I didn't have time to get ready.

中譯：他這麼倉促通知開會，害得我根本沒時間準備。

40. understand 瞭解，諒解（動詞）

例句：I hope the passengers understand why we canceled the train.

中譯：我希望旅客都諒解我們為什麼取消這班火車。

 understanding 理解（名詞）

例句：According to my understanding, the violence in the city will continue.

中譯：根據我的理解，城市暴力還會繼續。

understanding 體諒的，通情達理的（形容詞）

例句：Thank you for being such an understanding husband.

中譯：謝謝你這麼體諒人的丈夫。

41. message 音訊、消息（名詞）

例句：Young people today communicate mainly through the Internet and text messaging.

中譯：現在年輕人主要用網路和傳簡訊交談。

例句：He's not here right now. Can I take a message?

中譯：他現在不在，需要留言嗎？

Exercises
練習題

I. Multiple Choice 選擇題

1. (　　) I don't understand the _____ meaning of this word.

　　(a) develop　(b) available　(c) exact

2. (　　) I _____ for taking so long to answer your email.

　　(a) message　(b) apologize　(c) trouble

3. (　　) I was wondering if you could attend our _____ in the autumn.

　　(a) conference　(b) confirmation　(c) proposal

4. (　　) The doctor _____ that she was pregnant（懷孕了）.

　　(a) proposed　(b) followed　(c) confirmed

5. (　　) How much _____ have we made this week on the project?

　　(a) progress　(b) notice　(c) develop

6. (　　) I _____ if he will cancel our meeting.

　　(a) propose　(b) notice　(c) wonder

7. (　　) I am _____ that I may not be able to understand your proposed plan.

　　(a) afraid　(b) wondering　(c) available

8. (　　) They were interested in our products, but there was no _____.

　　(a) short notice　(b) cancellation　(c) follow-up

9. (　　) The food stand is very famous in our _____

　　(a) team　(b) neighborhood　(c) notice

10. (　　) His idea has not been fully _____ yet.

　　(a) apologized　(b) canceled　(c) developed

II. Fill in the Blank 請選適當的字填入空格中，沒有用到的字請劃掉

according to, conference, confirm, detail, propose, recognize

Marcus 正在組織一個 10 人小組會議，他寫信給同事 Stephanie，通知開會事宜：

Dear Stephanie,

Can you please 1._____ your attendance at tomorrow's committee meeting?

2._____ my notes, there should be 10 of us in the meeting. I 3._____ we meet at 3PM in the 3rd floor 4._____ room. However, I will send out the exact 5._____s once I hear back from all the members.

Thanks for your cooperation and see you tomorrow!
Marcus

III. Fill in the Blank 請選適當的字填入空格中，沒有用到的字請劃掉

apologize, attend, available, cancel, perhaps, progress, wonder

Summer 本約了老友 **Laura** 一起喝咖啡，沒想到臨時有事，只好寫封短信取消約會，並改約其他時間見面：

Hi Laura,

Terrible news! I have to 1._____ our coffee date today. I have a report to hand in by the end of today and I haven't made much 2._____ on it yet.

I 3._____ for the short notice. Are you 4._____ again tomorrow? 5._____ we can meet in the morning or early afternoon.

All the best,
Summer

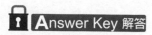 **A**nswer Key 解答

I. Multiple Choice

1	2	3	4	5	6	7	8	9	10
c	b	a	c	a	c	a	c	b	c

II. Fill in the Blank

1	2	3	4	5
confirm	According to	propose	conference	details

III. Fill in the Blank

1	2	3	4	5
cancel	progress	apologize	available	perhaps

Chapter 5

Sending an Invitation
邀約

邀請國外學者來台灣演講、邀請朋友出遊或聚餐、邀請業者參加商展……，用 **Globish** 單字表中的一些單字，便可寫成一封言詞懇切、禮貌周到的邀請函。

I. Inviting a Famous International Speaker to a Taiwanese Conference（Email Version）

邀請國際知名人士來台當國際會議主講者（電子郵件篇）

Roy Huang 是這場國際會議的籌備會主任，他寫了封電子郵件邀請 Lindsay Bell
教授來台為國際會議的開幕式演講：

🎧 34

Dear **Professor** Lindsay Bell,

I would like to **formally** invite you to **deliver** the **opening** speech at Hua Tung Bank's conference in Taipei, Taiwan, on November 12, 2012.

The title of this year's conference is "Crossing **Borders**: How To **Expand** Your Business in the **Age** of Globalization." This is the conference's 4th year and we hope to make it the best yet. We expect over 500 guests from across **various industries** and from around the world to attend this five-day-long **event**.

As a highly **experienced** and **influential figure** in global **trading**, we believe you would **offer** an interesting **angle** on how businesses can **face** the **challenges** of the 21st **century**. You will have between 45 and 60 minutes to speak.

We **truly** hope you will **accept** our invitation. Please send your answer as soon as possible so we can confirm the **remaining** event details.

Thank you in advance,

Roy Huang
Conference Director
Hua Tung Bank
+02-1234-5678
rhuang@htbank.com.tw

中譯

Lindsay Bell 教授，您好，

我正式邀請您參加 2012 年 11 月 12 日在台灣台北舉行的華東銀行貿易大會，並為我們的開幕式做一場演講。

今年會議的主題是：超越國界，全球化的時代裡，如何擴展商機。這是我們第四年舉辦此會議，我希望這次能辦得最好。

您是全球貿易界經驗豐富且極具影響力的人物，我們相信您一定可以為企業界在如何面對 21 世紀的挑戰的議題上提供有趣的視角。您演講的時間是 45 到 60 分鐘。

我們懇切地希望您能接受我們的邀約。請儘快給我們回音，我們好敲定其他的活動細節。

謝謝。

Roy Huang 敬上

Globish
單字

🎧 35

1. famous 聞名的、著名的（形容詞）

例句：The college is famous for its science program.

中譯：這間大學以理科著名。

2. professor 教授（名詞）

例句：She was an assistant professor, then an associate professor, and now she is a full professor.

中譯：他先是助理教授，再升為副教授，現在則是教授。

3. form 表格（名詞）

例句：Please fill out the form before you borrow the book.

中譯：請先填好表格再借書。

 formal 正式的（形容詞）

例句：We have to use the right tone when writing a formal letter.

中譯：我們得用正確的語調寫一封正式的信函。

formally 正式地（副詞）

例句：You had better dress formally for this ceremony.

中譯：參加這個慶典，你最好穿正式一點。

4. deliver 投遞、發表正式的演講（動詞）

例句：When are you going to deliver this parcel?

中譯：你何時遞送這個包裹？

例句：The president is going to deliver an important speech on Monday.

中譯：總統星期一要發表重要的演講。

 delivery 遞送（名詞）

例句：We will provide door-to-door delivery service.

中譯：我們將提供「一趟到家」的遞送服務。

delivery man 送貨員

例句：The delivery man will arrive at your apartment in 10 minutes.

中譯：送貨員十分鐘之內會到你的公寓。

5. open 開門、開市（動詞）

例句：When does the stock market open?

中譯：股票市場何時開市？

opening 開場、開幕（名詞）

例句：What time is the opening of the ball game?

中譯：球賽幾點鐘開場？

6. border 邊界（名詞）

例句：The border between those two countries is not peaceful.

中譯：這兩國的邊界不太平靜。

7. expand 擴展、擴張（動詞）

例句：Last year we expanded our company's business by 50%.

中譯：去年我們擴展了公司的業務達 50% 左右。

 expansion 擴展（名詞）

例句：The quick expansion program has failed.

中譯：急速擴張的計畫已經失敗了。

8. age 年齡、時代（名詞）

例句：Which age group is this product designed for?

中譯：這個產品是為哪一個年齡層設計的？

例句：Communication is important in the age of globalization.

中譯：通訊在全球化時代是非常重要的。

 aging 老化（形容詞）

例句：Taiwan's aging society has some severe challenges ahead.

中譯：台灣高齡化的社會將面一些嚴峻的挑戰。

9. vary 有不同、有變化（動詞）

例句：Aging problems vary from town to town in Taiwan.

中譯：台灣每個城鎮的高齡化問題各有不同。

various 不同的（形容詞）

例句：The government used various methods to solve the aging problem.

中譯：政府用了不同方法解決高齡化的問題。

a variety of 多種的

例句：People exercise for a variety of reasons.

中譯：人們做運動，出於多種理由。

10. industry 工業，業界（名詞）

例句：Business in the publishing industry is very slow right now.

中譯：出版業的生意目前很不景氣。

例句：Steel and metal factories belong to heavy industry.

中譯：鋼鐵和金屬工廠屬於重工業。

 industrious 勤勞的、勤奮工作的（形容詞）

例句：This popular government officer is an industrious person.

中譯：這位有名望的政府官員是位非常勤奮工作的人。

11. event 事件、節目（名詞）

例句：It is a shame that no one cares about this important event.

中譯：真可惜，居然沒有人關心這麼重要的事件。

12. experience 經驗（名詞）

例句：We cannot hire him because he lacks work experience.

中譯：我們不能聘用他，因為他缺少工作經驗。

experience 經歷（動詞）

例句：We experienced a brief power outage during the storm yesterday.

中譯：昨天暴風期間我們經歷了短暫的停電。

 experienced 有經驗的（形容詞）

例句：We need an experienced guide for the foreign visitors.

中譯：我們需要一位有經驗的導遊來帶外國旅客。

13. influence 影響（動詞）

例句：The bad weather will influence our food industry's business.

中譯：壞天氣將影響我們食品業的生意。

influence 影響（名詞）

例句：She has huge influence in Parliament.

中譯：她在國會裡有很大的影響力。

 influential 有影響力的（形容詞）

例句：She is an influential figure in politics.

中譯：她在政界是頗具影響力的人物。

14. figure 人物、角色（名詞）

例句：Who is the most important figure in your industry?

中譯：誰是你們業界裡最重要的人物？

 figure out 想出（動詞）

例句：Can you figure out a better solution to improve this terrible situation?

中譯：你能想出一個更好的解決辦法來改善這個糟糕的情況嗎？

15. **trade** 交易、商業、貿易（名詞）

例句：Two countries just signed a trade agreement.

中譯：兩個國家剛簽署了一份貿易同意書。

trade 交易（動詞）

例句：I just traded in my old Ford for a new Toyota.

中譯：我剛用我的舊福特車，抵新買的豐田汽車的一些花費。

> **trading** 商業、貿易的（形容詞）
>
> 例句：She just got promoted in a trading company.
>
> 中譯：她在貿易公司剛被升遷。

16. **offer** 提供、出價（動詞）

例句：I offered NT$500 million for his old studio apartment.

中譯：我出價 500 萬台幣買他舊的套房。

offer 機會（名詞）

例句：I accepted the job offer, but my friend turned it down.

中譯：我接受了這個工作機會，但我的朋友拒絕了。

17. **angle** 角度（名詞）

例句：We have to see things from a different angle.

中譯：我們必須從不同的角度來看事情。

18. **face** 面對、正視（動詞）

例句：We can't just act like nothing is wrong; we have to face the reality.

中譯：我們不能假裝天下太平；我們得面對現實。

19. **challenge** 挑戰（動詞）

例句：He doesn't like anyone to challenge his authority.

中譯：他不喜歡任何人挑戰他的權威。

challenge 挑戰、衝突（名詞）

例句：He always avoids facing the challenges.

中譯：他總是避開正面的衝突。

20. century 世紀

例句：There have been a lot of new research projects since the start of the 21st century.

中譯：21 世紀一開始就有許多新的研究計畫案。

21. true 真的（形容詞）

例句：This is a true story, not fiction.

中譯：這是真實的故事，不是小說。

 truly 真的（副詞）

例句：I am truly sorry. I didn't mean to hurt you.

中譯：我真的很抱歉，我不是有意傷害你的。

22. accept 接受（動詞）

例句：I accept your apology.

中譯：我接受你的道歉。

23. remain 保持（動詞）

例句：My brother remained single for many years after his divorce.

中譯：離婚多年之後我哥哥仍保持單身。

 remaining 剩下的、其餘的（形容詞）

例句：We will deal with the remaining problems next time.

中譯：我們下回再處理剩下來的麻煩事。

II. Inviting a Guest to a Traditional Taiwanese Meal （Email Version）

邀請來訪客人嚐嚐台灣傳統餐點（電子郵件篇）

Roy Huang 很高興收到 Bell 教授允諾來台灣演講的回信，他想邀請 Bell 教授演講完後享用台灣料理：

🎧 36

Dear Professor Bell,

Thank you again for agreeing to speak at our conference in November.

While you are in Taipei, I wonder if you would be interested in letting us take you out for a **traditional** Taiwanese dinner. **Compared** with other Chinese meals, Taiwanese dishes **taste** much **lighter** and are better for your health.

Are you available on Tuesday, November 13? We could meet you in the hotel lobby at around 7:00PM.

There is a very popular restaurant about two **blocks** away from your hotel that I **suggest** we try. It is famous for its **smoked** fish. I **guarantee** you will leave **satisfied**!

All the best,
Roy Huang

 中譯

Bell 教授，您好，

我們再次感謝您答應在 11 月的會議上為我們演講。

您在台北時，我想知道您是否有興趣讓我們帶您去吃傳統台灣式的晚餐，與其他中